# Miss Fox's Class Gets It Wrong

Eileen Spinelli   Illustrated by Anne Kennedy

Albert Whitman & Company, Chicago, Illinois

Also by Eileen Spinelli and Anne Kennedy:

*Peace Week in Miss Fox's Class*
*Miss Fox's Class Goes Green*
*Miss Fox's Class Earns a Field Trip*
*Miss Fox's Class Gets Fit*

Library of Congress Cataloging-in-Publication Data

Spinelli, Eileen.
Miss Fox's class gets it wrong / by Eileen Spinelli ; illustrated by Anne Kennedy.
p. cm.
Summary: Miss Fox's class assumes their teacher's association with a police officer is something other than what it really is.
ISBN 978-0-8075-5165-3 (hardcover)
[1. Gossip—Fiction. 2. Schools—Fiction. 3. Animals—Fiction.]  I. Kennedy, Anne, ill. II. Title.
PZ7.S7566Mhp 2012
[E]—dc2

The design is by Carol Gildar.

For more information about Albert Whitman & Company,
please visit our web site at www.albertwhitman.com.

To my friends Nancy, Peggy, Pat, and Mary.—E.S.

To dear and thoughtful Mindy.—A.K.

One morning, Officer Blue Fox came to Miss Fox's classroom. He spoke to the students about safety.

"Wear your helmets when riding a bike."

"Always walk with a buddy."

"Never play in the street."

Afterward, Frog had a question. "Have you ever arrested anyone, Officer Blue Fox?"

"Yes, I have," he replied. "But I'd rather not. I'd like everyone to be a good citizen."

A week later, Young Bear saw something that worried him. He saw Officer Blue Fox stop Miss Fox on her bike. Miss Fox must have disobeyed one of the safety rules.

Young Bear told his classmates.

"Oh, my," said Mouse. "I hope Principal Moose doesn't find out."

Then one Saturday, Frog saw Officer Blue Fox leading
Miss Fox into the police station.

On Monday, he told the other students, "I think Miss Fox
was arrested!"

But Miss Fox walked into the classroom as usual—smiling. Bunny whispered, "Officer Blue Fox must have given Miss Fox another chance."

As time went on, the students noticed Miss Fox and Officer Blue Fox together. Often.

The students were puzzled. Why was Miss Fox in so much trouble with the law?

Miss Fox believed in peace. And in recycling. And in working hard for the things you wanted.

Miss Fox was an excellent citizen. Wasn't she?

Two worrisome things happened in the same weekend.

Raccoon and Bunny had collected old books from their neighbors. They were taking the books to the library sale when Bunny exclaimed, "Look! There's Miss Fox coming out of the drugstore!"

Raccoon looked. All she saw was someone wearing a red hat and big, fancy sunglasses. "I don't see her."

"Sure you do," said Bunny. "That's her with the hat and sunglasses."

"Why do you think she's wearing sunglasses?" asked Raccoon. "It's cloudy out today."

They talked about it all the way to the library.

Later, Frog and Squirrel came to buy books at the sale.
They had seen Miss Fox, too.

Frog told Raccoon, "Miss Fox was putting a suitcase
in her car."

"We think she's going away," added Squirrel.

"I wonder where," said Raccoon.

The students stared at one another.

Then on Monday morning came the clincher. As the students headed for their seats, every one of them saw something on Miss Fox's desk. It was a travel brochure. It showed palm trees and white beaches. Three words were splashed across it: YOUR HAWAIIAN GETAWAY!

The students were buzzing like bees when Miss Fox
entered the room. She was not alone. Officer Blue Fox was
with her!

"Students," she said. "I have big news—"
Young Bear jumped up. "No! We don't want to hear it!"
Miss Fox looked bewildered. "You don't?"
"No, Miss Fox," said Young Bear. "You don't have to confess
to us. We know all about it."
"You do?" said Miss Fox.

Mouse piped up. "We know Officer Blue Fox stopped you on your bike one day."

"And Frog saw Officer Blue Fox taking you into the police station," said Raccoon.

Bunny hopped on her seat. "We know you're in trouble with the law, Miss Fox. But we don't care. We still love you."

"We'll visit you in jail!" Mouse cried out.

"We know you were planning your getaway to Hawaii," said Squirrel.

"With your suitcase and your disguise," said Frog.

"My disguise?" said Miss Fox.

"Your red hat and big, fancy sunglasses," explained Bunny.

Suddenly, the only sound in the classroom was the laughter of Miss Fox and Officer Blue Fox.

"My dear, dear students," Miss Fox finally managed to say. She wiped tears from her eyes. "Yes, I'm going to Hawaii. That's why I bought the suitcase, the hat, and the sunglasses. But no, I'm not in trouble with the law."

She took Officer Blue Fox's hand. "Quite the opposite," she said. "Officer Blue Fox and I are getting married, and you're all invited! We are going to honeymoon in Hawaii!"

At first, the students were too stunned to speak. Then they went wild.

On the morning of the wedding, the students were even more excited. They dressed in their very, very best.

Next, they went to meet Custodian Mole. There was one more thing left to do.

It was time.

The wedding party arrived at the church. Custodian Mole helped Miss Fox off the bus. She was beautiful in her lacy wedding dress.

Racoon handed Miss Fox her wedding bouquet.

Miss Fox gathered her students around her.
"This is your big day, Miss Fox," said Young Bear.
Mouse grinned. "We're glad we don't have to visit you
in jail after all."

"And that reminds me," said Miss Fox. "One lesson before I go. Use your imagination for your schoolwork—not for rumors and gossip. Make sure you have all the facts straight before you start telling stories about others."

She reached out to them. "Deal?"

"Deal!" they cried.

Principal Moose called out, "We're ready!" The wedding party
entered the church, which was filled with friends and family.
The organist played "The Wedding March."
Up front, Officer Blue Fox waited with a big smile.

"Okay, students of honor," said Miss Fox. "Here we go."
Two by two, the students marched down the aisle.
Last of all—on her parents' arms—came the bride.